COUNTING ELEPHANTS

by Dawn Young

Illustrated by Fermin Solis

RP | KIDS

PHILADELPHIA

Running Press Kids
Hachette Book Group
1290 Avenue of the Americas, New York, NY 10104
www.runningpress.com/rpkids
@RP_Kids

Printed in China

First Edition: March 2020

Published by Running Press Kids, an imprint of Perseus Books, LLC,
a subsidiary of Hachette Book Group, Inc. The Running Press Kids name
and logo is a trademark of the Hachette Book Group.

The Hachette Speakers Bureau provides a wide range of authors for speaking events.
To find out more, go to www.hachettespeakersbureau.com or call (866) 376-6591.

The publisher is not responsible for websites (or their content)
that are not owned by the publisher.

Print book cover and interior design by Frances J. Soo Ping Chow.

Library of Congress Control Number: 2018963235

ISBNs: 978-0-7624-6694-8 (hardcover), 978-0-7624-6693-1 (ebook),
978-0-7624-6774-7 (ebook), 978-0-7624-6775-4 (ebook)

1010

10 9 8 7 6 5 4 3 2 1

For John, whom I can always count on
and for Jace, Remi, and Rylee who make life magical!
—D.Y.

To Marisina, Noel, and Elena.
My favorite elephants.
—F.S.

Counter: Hello, there! Welcome to our counting book.

Magician: Counting book? You said we were going to do magic.

Counter: No, I said math.

Magician: But I don't want to do math. I want to do magic.

Counter: Our readers are here to do math.

Magician: I think they'd rather do magic . . .

Counter: Well, math *is* magical. Now, here we have 10 elephants.

Magician: Not anymore.

Counter: There were 10 elephants here. I saw them.

Magician: I turned one into a frog since he kept trying to take my wand. So now there are 1, 2, 3, 4, 5, 6, 7, 8, 9 elephants and— TA DA! —1 frog.

Counter: OK, enough with the hokey pocus. It's time to count. Here we have 9—

Magician: You mean 8? 8 elephants.

Counter: 8?

Magician: Yep. **PRESTO!** 1 is now peanut butter.

Counter: Peanut butter?!

Magician: I thought you might be hungry. Besides, elephants love peanut butter.

Counter: Umm, elephants love *peanuts* but . . . can we just count the 8 elephants?

Magician: Uh, 7 elephants, 1 frog, 1 jar of peanut butter, and—VOILÀ!— 1 jar of jelly because what's peanut butter without jelly?

Counter: Great, now you and your frog can hop away and have a peanut butter and jelly picnic while we count the 7 elephants.

Magician: For someone who loves math, you sure have trouble counting.

Magician: There are 6 elephants!

Counter: 6?! I saw 7 elephants.

Magician: There *were* 7 elephants, but now there are 6. Along with 1 frog, 1 jar of peanut butter, 1 jar of jelly, and—ABRACADABRA! —1 puppy.

Counter: A puppy?

Magician: I've always wanted a puppy.

Counter: Then go teach your puppy some tricks and we'll count the 6 elephants.

Magician: You mean *puppies.*

Counter: PUPPIES!!!???

Magician: Yeah, the little guy needed some friends to play with.

Counter: So, there are how many elephants?

Magician: 3.

Counter: *Only* 3 elephants?

Magician: And 1 frog, 1 jar of peanut butter, 1 jar of jelly, and 1, 2, 3, 4 adorable puppies.

Counter: Yes, they're cute, but we need to count the elephants. There are still 3, right?

Magician: Nope, just 1. After all, frogs need friends, too.

Counter: Fine, just PLEASE stop waving that wand so we can count the 1 elephant!

Magician: Too late. I just turned that one into a rabbit.

Counter: A rabbit?!?

Magician: Yes. What kind of magician would I be without a rabbit to pull out of my hat?

Counter: No! Wait! Stop! This is a book about—

Magician: And there you have it, kids. A book about magic! And 0 elephants, 1 jar of peanut butter, 1 jar of jelly, 1, 2, 3, 4 very cute puppies, 1, 2, 3 frogs, and 1 rabbit, who—uh oh—Won't. Come. Out. Of. His. Hat!

Counter: Now look what you've done. This book is a mess. The readers were counting on me!

Magician: You should have said so.

Counter: NO!!! They were counting on me to count elephants.

Magician: Oh!

Counter: UGH! YOU MAKE ME NUTS!

Magician: Okay! If you insist.

Counter: HELP! The whole herd is after me!

Magician: That's not a herd, it's only 1, 2, 3, 4, 5, 6, 7, 8, 9, 10 elephants.
Hey, you were right. There are 10 elephants. Ten *hungry* elephants.

Counter: Do something!

Magician: Oh nuts!

Counter: Whew. That was close!

Magician: What should we count next?

319010659812893